32044

E

IC

D1531497

Just Like Dora!

by Alison Inches
illustrated by Dave Aikins

PROPERTY OF
TRI-CITIES CHRISTIAN SCHOOLS
WESLEY CENTER

SCHOLASTIC INC.
New York Toronto London Auckland Sydney
Mexico City New Delhi Hong Kong Buenos Aires

Based on the TV series *Dora the Explorer*® as seen on Nick Jr.®

No part of this publication may be reproduced, stored in a retrieval system,
or transmitted in any form or by any means, electronic, mechanical, photocopying,
recording, or otherwise, without written permission of the publisher.
For information regarding permission, write to Simon Spotlight, Simon & Schuster Children's
Publishing Division, 1230 Avenue of the Americas, New York, NY 10020.

ISBN 0-439-76086-0

Copyright © 2005 by Viacom International Inc. NICKELODEON, NICK JR.,
Dora the Explorer, and all related titles, logos, and characters are trademarks of
Viacom International Inc. All rights reserved. Published by Scholastic Inc.,
557 Broadway, New York, NY 10012, by arrangement with Simon Spotlight,
Simon & Schuster Children's Publishing Division. SCHOLASTIC and associated
logos are trademarks and/or registered trademarks of Scholastic Inc.

12 11 10 9 8 7 6 5 4 3 2 1   5 6 7 8 9 10/0

Printed in the U.S.A.   23

First Scholastic printing, September 2005

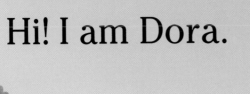

Hi! I am Dora.

Do you like surprises?

Then follow me!

Hop across the rocks!

Hop! Hop! Hop!

Splash in the water!

Just like me!

Row across the lake!

Row! Row! Row!

Slide down the hill!

Just like me!

Are we there yet?

Not yet!

Swing on the vines!

Swing! Swing! Swing!

Jump over the logs!

Just like me!

Here we are!

Guess what we see!

An ice-cream party!

Yummy!

We did it!